For Dad, who inspired this story

little bee books

An imprint of Bonnier Publishing Group
853 Broadway, New York, New York 10003
Text and illustration copyright © 2015 by Amy Husband.
First published in the United Kingdom by Top That Publishing Ltd.
This little bee books edition, 2015.
All rights reserved, including the right of reproduction in whole
or in part in any form. LITTLE BEE BOOKS is a trademark of
Bonnier Publishing Group.
Manufactured in Guangdong, China 1014 HH
First Edition 2 4 6 8 10 9 7 5 3 1
Library of Congress Control Number: 2015902905
ISBN 978-1-4998-0154-5

www.littlebeebooks.com
www.bonnierpublishing.com

The NOISY FOXES

by Amy HUSBAND

little bee books

In a **very noisy** house in a **very noisy** city lived three **noisy** foxes.

They spent
ALL DAY
being
very noisy . . .

mixing . . .

fixing . . .

hopping and
bopping . . .

banging
and
clanging.

"Wouldn't it be nice to be quiet sometimes?" asked Fox Number One.

"Perhaps we should move to the countryside," suggested Fox Number Two.

"What a good idea!" replied Fox Number Three.

So they packed up all of their **very noisy** things and caught the **very noisy** bus to find a place to live in the very quiet **countryside**.

whoo-whoo!

In a very quiet **wood** in the very quiet countryside, they met an owl.

"Whoo-whoo. Who are you?" hooted the owl.

"We are from the **very noisy** city, looking for a quiet place to live," replied Fox Number One. "Where do you live, Owl?"

"I live up here at the top of this very tall, very quiet tree," the owl said.

"Oh yes, it is very quiet, but it is too high for us," said Fox Number One. "We're scared!"

Next, in a very quiet meadow in the very quiet countryside, the **noisy** foxes met a mole, who popped up out of the ground.

"Hello, Mole. We are from the **noisy** city looking for a quiet place to live. Can you help us?" asked Fox Number Two.

"Oh yes, I live in a very quiet place," replied the mole. "Follow me and I'll show you."

In a very quiet clearing in the very quiet countryside, the **noisy** foxes met a frog.

"Ribbit, ribbit. What do you three **noisy** foxes want?" the frog asked.

"We are looking for a quiet place to live," said Fox Number Three. "Where do you live, Frog?"

"Come with me and I'll show you," replied the frog.

"I live here in this very quiet pond," said the frog.

"Oh yes, it is very quiet indeed, but it is too wet for us," said Fox Number Three. "And we can't swim!"

So the three **noisy** foxes kept searching for a very, very long time, and they ended up in the quietest part of the countryside, a long, long way from the **very noisy** city. As they ventured along the very quiet path, they met a badger.

"Hello, Badger. We are looking for a quiet place to live," said the **noisy** foxes. "Can you help us? We have looked everywhere."

"Yes, of course. Follow me," replied the badger.

"This is where I live," said the badger.
"It is the quietest place in all of the countryside."

"Oh yes, it really is very quiet, and very lovely.
It might just be the perfect place," said the
noisy foxes. "But . . .

. . . it is just TOO quiet!"

The **noisy** foxes were tired of being quiet, so they started to make some noise! As they banged and clanged and chittered and chattered, a quiet little mouse scurried up to them.

"What is all this noise about?" asked the quiet little mouse.

"We need a place to live, but it can't be too high, it can't be too dark, it can't be too wet, and it definitely can't be too quiet," replied the **noisy** foxes.

"I know the perfect place,"
squeaked the mouse. "Follow me."

"Well done, little mouse. This really is the perfect place!"

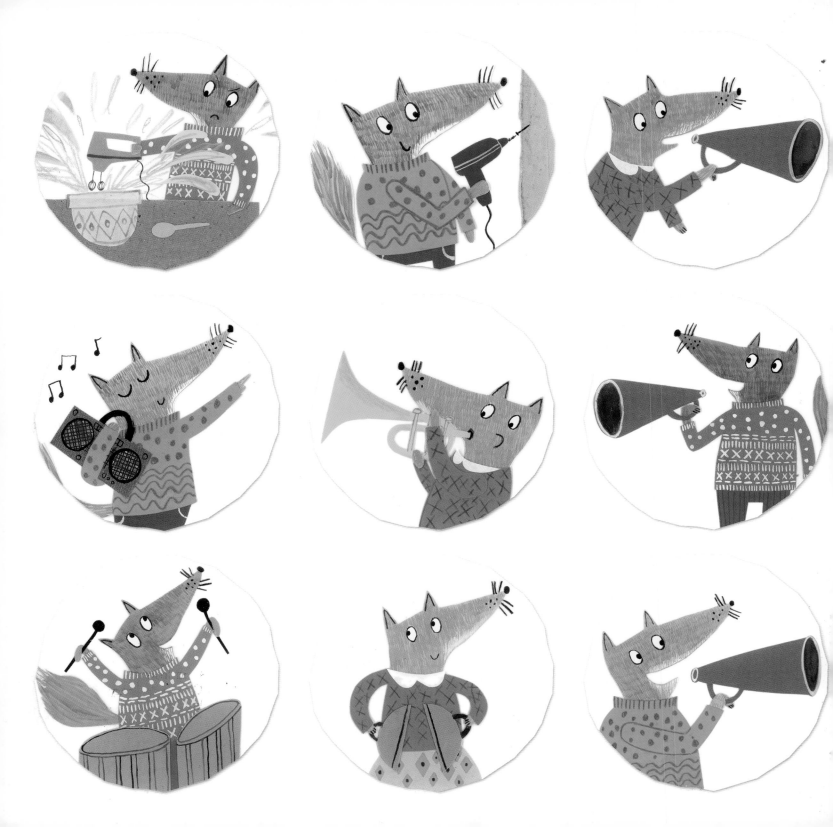